THIS BOOK BELONGS TO

....

THE TALE
OF
MR. JEREMY FISHER

THE TALE OF

MR. JEREMY FISHER

BY

BEATRIX POTTER

Author of
" The Tale of Peter Rabbit," &c.

FREDERICK WARNE

The reproductions in this book have been made using
the most modern electronic scanning methods from entirely
new transparencies of Beatrix Potter's original watercolours.
They enable Beatrix Potter's skill as an artist to be appreciated
as never before, not even during her own lifetime.

FREDERICK WARNE

Published by the Penguin Group
27 Wrights Lane, London W8 5TZ, England
Penguin Books USA Inc., 375 Hudson Street, New York, New York 10014, USA
Penguin Books Australia Ltd, Ringwood, Victoria, Australia
Penguin Books Canada Ltd, 10 Alcorn Avenue, Toronto, Ontario, Canada M4V 3B2
Penguin Books (NZ) Ltd, 182-190 Wairau Road, Auckland 10, New Zealand

Penguin Books Ltd, Registered Offices: Harmondsworth, Middlesex, England

First published 1906
Published with new reproductions 1987
This paperback edition first published 1991

Printed and bound in Great Britain by
William Clowes Limited, Beccles and London

FOR
STEPHANIE
FROM
COUSIN B.

8

ONCE upon a time there was a frog called Mr. Jeremy Fisher; he lived in a little damp house amongst the buttercups at the edge of a pond.

THE water was all slippy-sloppy in the larder and in the back passage.

But Mr. Jeremy liked getting his feet wet; nobody ever scolded him, and he never caught a cold!

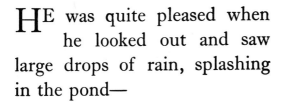

HE was quite pleased when
he looked out and saw
large drops of rain, splashing
in the pond—

"I WILL get some worms and go fishing and catch a dish of minnows for my dinner," said Mr. Jeremy Fisher. "If I catch more than five fish, I will invite my friends Mr. Alderman Ptolemy Tortoise and Sir Isaac Newton. The Alderman, however, eats salad."

MR. JEREMY put on a macintosh, and a pair of shiny goloshes ; he took his rod and basket, and set off with enormous hops to the place where he kept his boat.

THE boat was round and green, and very like the other lily-leaves. It was tied to a water-plant in the middle of the pond.

M R. JEREMY took a reed
pole, and pushed the
boat out into open water. "I
know a good place for minnows," said Mr. Jeremy
Fisher.

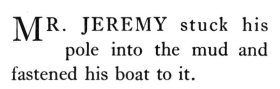

MR. JEREMY stuck his
pole into the mud and
fastened his boat to it.

Then he settled himself
cross-legged and arranged his
fishing tackle. He had the
dearest little red float. His
rod was a tough stalk of
grass, his line was a fine long
white horse-hair, and he tied
a little wriggling worm at the
end.

24

THE rain trickled down his back, and for nearly an hour he stared at the float.

"This is getting tiresome, I think I should like some lunch," said Mr. Jeremy Fisher.

HE punted back again amongst the water-plants, and took some lunch out of his basket.

"I will eat a butterfly sandwich, and wait till the shower is over," said Mr. Jeremy Fisher.

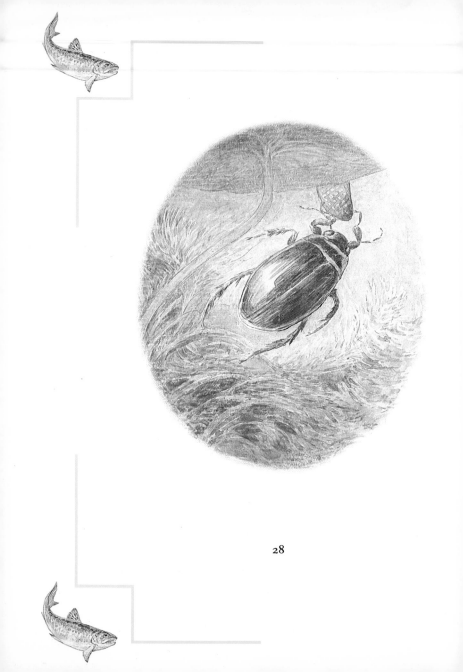

A GREAT big water-beetle
came up underneath the
lily leaf and tweaked the toe
of one of his goloshes.

Mr. Jeremy crossed his legs
up shorter, out of reach, and
went on eating his sandwich.

ONCE or twice something moved about with a rustle and a splash amongst the rushes at the side of the pond.

"I trust that is not a rat," said Mr. Jeremy Fisher; " I think I had better get away from here."

MR. JEREMY shoved the boat out again a little way, and dropped in the bait. There was a bite almost directly; the float gave a tremendous bobbit!

"A minnow! a minnow! I have him by the nose!" cried Mr. Jeremy Fisher, jerking up his rod.

BUT what a horrible sur-
prise! Instead of a
smooth fat minnow, Mr.
Jeremy landed little Jack
Sharp the stickleback, covered
with spines!

36

THE stickleback floundered about the boat, pricking and snapping until he was quite out of breath. Then he jumped back into the water.

A^{ND} a shoal of other little
    fishes put their heads
out, and laughed at Mr.
Jeremy Fisher.

39

40

AND while Mr. Jeremy sat disconsolately on the edge of his boat—sucking his sore fingers and peering down into the water—a *much* worse thing happened; a really *frightful* thing it would have been, if Mr. Jeremy had not been wearing a macintosh!

A GREAT big enormous trout came up—ker-pflop-p-p-p! with a splash—and it seized Mr. Jeremy with a snap, "Ow! Ow! Ow!"—and then it turned and dived down to the bottom of the pond!

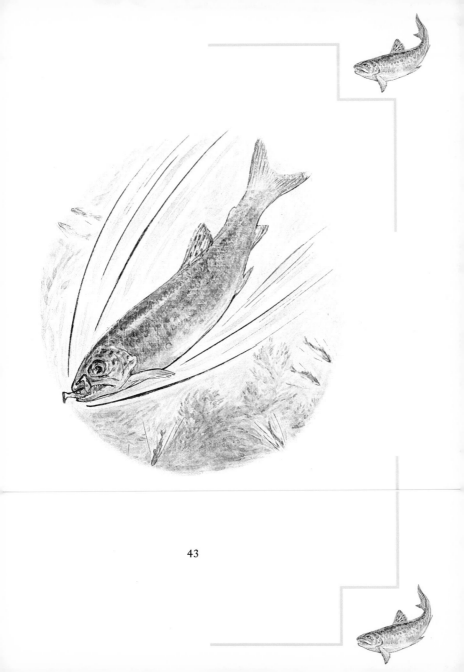

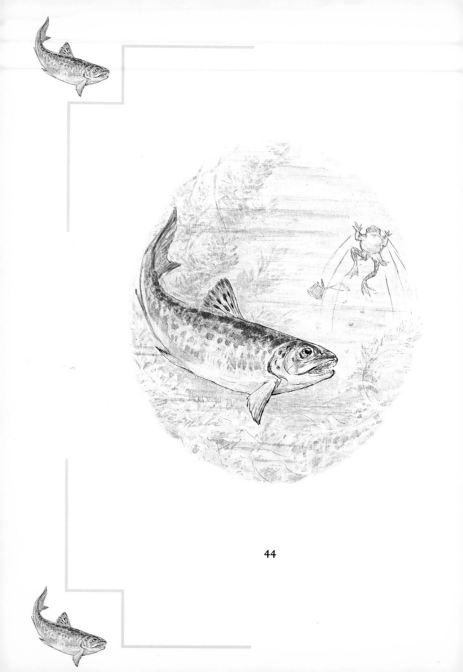

BUT the trout was so displeased with the taste of the macintosh, that in less than half a minute it spat him out again; and the only thing it swallowed was Mr. Jeremy's goloshes.

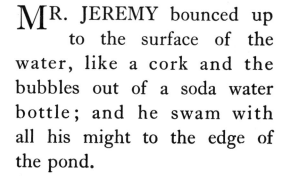

MR. JEREMY bounced up
to the surface of the
water, like a cork and the
bubbles out of a soda water
bottle; and he swam with
all his might to the edge of
the pond.

HE scrambled out on the first bank he came to, and he hopped home across the meadow with his mac- intosh all in tatters.

"WHAT a mercy that was not a pike!" said Mr. Jeremy Fisher. "I have lost my rod and basket; but it does not much matter, for I am sure I should never have dared to go fishing again!"

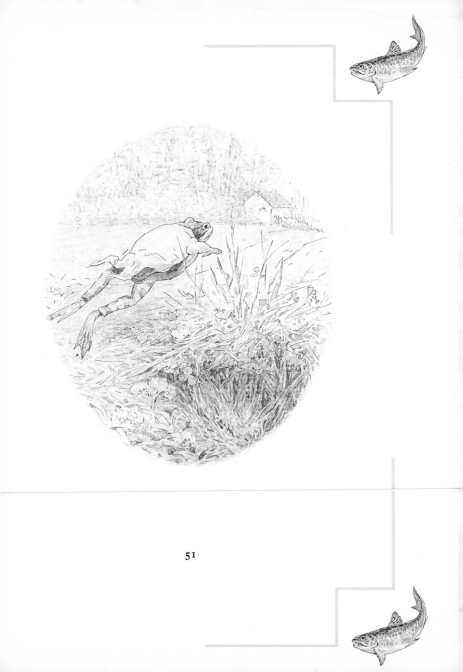

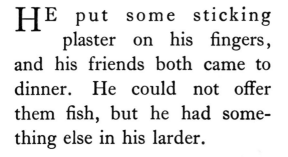

HE put some sticking
plaster on his fingers,
and his friends both came to
dinner. He could not offer
them fish, but he had something else in his larder.

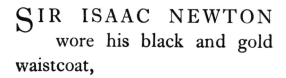

S IR ISAAC NEWTON wore his black and gold waistcoat,

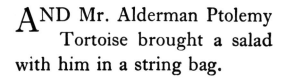

ND Mr. Alderman Ptolemy
Tortoise brought a salad
with him in a string bag.

AND instead of a nice dish of minnows—they had a roasted grasshopper with lady-bird sauce; which frogs consider a beautiful treat; but *I* think it must have been nasty!

THE END

Some other Beatrix Potter books

The Complete Tales of Beatrix Potter

The Miniature World of Peter Rabbit:
12–Copy Box

Beatrix Potter's Countryside Book

The World of Peter Rabbit Sticker Book

The World of Peter Rabbit Postcard Book

My Photograph Album: a
Beatrix Potter Keepsake

Beatrix Potter Posters